The BIGGEST Thing of All

By
Kathryn Thurman

Illustrated by
Romina Galotta

UPS!DE DOWN BOOKS

On summer days, Lily helps Grandma in her garden.

Lily loves the poppies. Grandma loves the lavender.
Lily loves Grandma.
And Grandma, of course, loves Lily.

There's a lot of work to do when everything is
growing. Grandpa, Mama and Papa all help out.

Even Grandma's cat, Oliver, does his part!

One day, in front of the prize-winning roses, Grandpa tells Lily that *everything* is a part of something bigger. Grandma turns a rock over.

'See: one ant is part of a whole colony,' says Grandpa.

Together, they think of more:
One bee is part of a hive.
One butterfly is part of a swarm.
'One bird is part of a flock,' says Lily.
'Now what can be bigger than that?'

'Hmm,' says Grandpa,
rubbing his chin.

At night, they look up at the sky.

'The moon, the stars, and the Earth
are part of the universe,' says Lily.

'Now, that's **really big!**' says Grandma.

Lily agrees.
She's not sure there could be anything bigger.

Soon, leaves turn orange. The wind gets chilly.
And Grandma becomes too tired to work in the
garden. Lily does her part by picking *all* the
lavender for her. Grandpa helps, too.

They bring the harvest in.

The house bursts with the scent
of Grandma's favourite flower.

The rain comes. The whole family stays inside.
Mama and Papa make lavender lemonade and lavender tea . . .
and brownies sweetened with love.

Still, Lily misses the sunshine.
If only the rain would go away.

Then Grandpa reminds her. 'Everything is a part of something bigger.
Even one raindrop becomes part of the sea.'

Water puddles in the garden. And more and more, Grandma stays in bed.

Everyone spends time with her.

Each day, Lily draws her pictures.

One twig is part of a tree.
One petal is part of a rose.
One stone is part of a path.

one
twig is
part of
a tree

my
house

But then, one day . . .
Grandma's gone.

The wind blows
a lonely howl.

Mama and Papa try to hug Lily.

But she runs outside into the cold, cold rain and slams the garden gate.

This is where the poppies used to be.
She stomps the mud with her foot.
This is where the butterflies used to land.

Lily smacks a bush.
And then she cries.

For a long time, nothing feels the same.

Oliver needs snuggles.
Lily has decided she needs snuggles now, too.

And Grandpa stays in his room for days.

One Grandpa was part of a pair.

Winter comes early. Snow flutters
and swirls. Oliver doesn't chase
mice and Grandpa doesn't smile.

We need something sweet, Lily thinks.

But even brownies and lavender
tea don't make them feel better.

When the snow finally
melts, Lily can see
Grandma's garden again.

It's a mess!

She makes a plan.

Once she begins, everyone wants to help.
Lily and Oliver check the garden every day.

Oliver finds a slippery worm.

Lily finds one ant.

She starts to worry.

What if Grandma's garden doesn't come back?

What if Grandpa doesn't smile again?

But then she remembers . . .
Everything is a part of something bigger.

Soon, roses, poppies and lavender return.
And, look – a hedgehog!

But Lily's plan isn't finished.
Mama hangs lanterns.
Papa sets up the tables.

Things look so cheerful . . .
Grandpa can hardly believe his eyes!

Lily walks with him into the deepest part of the garden.
She reminds him that *everything* is a part of something bigger.

'Even us. One Grandpa, one Lily, one Mama and Papa,
one Oliver, too . . . we're *all* part of a family.'

Grandpa finally smiles.

Friends start to arrive. They share stories about Lily's Grandma. They eat brownies and drink lavender lemonade – Grandma's favourite.

Lily can feel Grandma's love all around them.
It even smells like Grandma.

'Grandma's love is so big,' she tells Grandpa.
'I don't think there's a place it can't reach.'

Grandpa squeezes Lily's hand. 'Now *that's* big.'

And she and Grandpa
both agree . . .

. . . love is the biggest thing of all.

To everyone on this beautiful planet; love is never lost. - KT

To my grandparents: Lala, José, Popona and Lolo. - RG

UPS!DE DOWN BOOKS

First published in Great Britain 2021 by Upside Down Books
an imprint of Trigger Publishing

Trigger Publishing is a trading style of Shaw Callaghan Ltd & Shaw Callaghan 23 USA, INC.
The Foundation Centre
Navigation House, 48 Millgate, Newark
Nottinghamshire NG24 4TS UK
www.triggerpublishing.com

British Library Cataloguing in Publication Data

A CIP catalogue record for this book is available upon request
from the British Library

ISBN: 978-1-78956-117-3

Kathryn Thurman and Romina Galotta have asserted their rights under the Copyright,
Design and Patents Act 1988 to be identified as the author of this work

Designed by Kathryn Davies
Printed and bound in China
Paper from responsible sources

At Upside Down Books, we are committed to helping children understand emotionally challenging situations. Grief, an emotion we all experience, can seem difficult to explain to children. A gentle and poignant story like *The Biggest Thing of All* explains death and loss through nature and the connectedness of the world around us. While the death of Lily's grandma is incredibly sad, this book shows that grief can be a unifying force within a family and that life can still be celebrated after it is gone. Young readers will identify with Lily and her sadness, and will discover a safe way to understand and process grief.

Lauren Callaghan

Consultant Clinical Psychologist,
Co-founder and Clinical Director of Trigger Publishing